The Adventures of JIMMY NEUTRON BOY GENIUS

D0565189

Battle of the Band

by Steven Banks   illustrated by Barry Goldberg

based on the teleplay by Spencer Green

Simon Spotlight/Nickelodeon
New York   London   Toronto   Sydney   Singapore

Based on the TV series *The Adventures of Jimmy Neutron, Boy Genius*® as seen on Nickelodeon®

SIMON SPOTLIGHT
An imprint of Simon & Schuster Children's Publishing Division
1230 Avenue of the Americas, New York, NY 10020
Copyright © 2003 Viacom International Inc. All rights reserved. NICKELODEON,
The Adventures of Jimmy Neutron, Boy Genius, and all related titles, logos, and
characters are trademarks of Viacom International Inc. All rights reserved,
including the right of reproduction in whole or in part in any form.
SIMON SPOTLIGHT and colophon are registered trademarks of Simon & Schuster.
Manufactured in the United States of America
First Edition 10 9 8 7 6 5 4 3 2 1
ISBN 0-689-85299-1

Brrring! The school bell sounded and Jimmy and his classmates rushed to gather their things.

"Wait!" shouted Miss Fowl. "Don't forget the talent contest is on Monday! And first prize is this big, gold trophy!"

Jimmy Neutron and his friends Carl and Sheen were determined to win the contest.

"I'm gonna blow nose bubbles!" Carl said proudly.

"Tough break, Carl," said Sheen. "I'm going to win with my famous water-spitting routine!"

"Well, I was going to solve algebra problems in Latin," Jimmy said, "but I think we have a better shot at the trophy if we do something together. Something a little more *exciting*."

"Hey, Nerdtron!" called Cindy Vortex. "Don't get any big ideas about that contest, 'cause *we're* going to win!"

"Yeah, we're going to do a dance routine," Libby added. "Ready? Hit it!" Cindy and Libby hopped onto the cafeteria table and began to dance. Their feet moved so fast, the boys could hardly see them.

"Beat that!" Cindy said, huffing and out of breath.

Jimmy looked around the room, trying to come up with an idea. "Our . . . um . . . our rock band is going to play!"

Cindy and Libby laughed. "You lamebrains have a rock band? That'll be the funniest thing we ever saw!"

"But, Jimmy, we don't have a band!" whispered Sheen.

"We don't even know how to play any instruments!" said Carl.

Jimmy smiled. "That's what *you* think," he said. "They don't call me boy genius for nothing!"

Jimmy, Carl, and Sheen went to Jimmy's lab to check out his latest invention: The Neutronic Atomic Mind Instrument. Jimmy handed Sheen an electric bass guitar and set Carl up behind a drum set.

"You see, I installed a computer inside each instrument," said Jimmy. "All you do is *think* the music, and the instrument plays it for you!"

Sheen strummed a chord on his bass guitar. "Wow! I rock!"

Carl began to bang away on the drums. "I can play the drums!" he yelled. "Somebody call my mom!"

"We'll show Cindy and Libby!" Jimmy shouted. "That trophy is ours!"

Cindy and Libby were walking Cindy's dog when they heard the music coming from Jimmy's garage.

"Oh, no!" Cindy cried. "Nerdtron actually rocks!"

"We'd better go practice!" said Libby.

"I have seen the future of rock 'n' roll!" said Sheen. "And it is us!"

Jimmy nodded his head. "This is just the beginning, boys. After we win the contest, we could become real rock stars!" They all closed their eyes and imagined themselves performing on a giant stage.

Carl imagined that he was playing the drums, surrounded by his favorite animals in the world . . . llamas.

Sheen imagined that his favorite superhero, Ultra Lord, flew onto the stage and said, "Once again your bass playing has made the world safe for democracy!"

Jimmy imagined that Cindy and Libby were begging for his autograph.

Then the trouble began. Carl wanted to sing a song about llamas. Sheen wanted to sing about Ultra Lord. And Jimmy wanted to sing about Albert Einstein.

Then Carl wanted to play a drum solo. Sheen wanted to play a bass solo. And Jimmy wanted a solo too.

Carl said they should wear funny makeup on their faces. Sheen wanted them to wear leather jackets. But Jimmy just wanted to play music. They argued so much that they didn't rehearse at all.

The next night was the talent contest.

Cindy and Libby danced onstage while Jimmy and his friends waited backstage.

"If I don't get my drum solo, I'm not going on!" declared Carl.

"Good! We don't need you!" yelled Sheen. "More time for my song about Ultra Lord!"

"We're *not* singing about Ultra Lord!" Jimmy shouted.

"Jimmy, I can't believe I let you be in my band!" screamed Sheen as Carl nodded in agreement.

"*Your* band?!" exclaimed Jimmy. "If it wasn't for my instruments, you guys would be blowing nose bubbles and spitting water!"

"Oh, yeah? Here's what we think of your instruments!" cried Sheen as he and Carl tossed their instruments out the window.

Jimmy shook his head. "We're best friends, and ever since we started this band, we've been fighting."

"I'd rather be friends than rock stars," said Carl.

"Me too," agreed Sheen.

Just then Miss Fowl popped her head in from behind the curtain. "Okay, boys. You're on!"

"What are we going to do?" Sheen asked in a panic.

"Brain blast!" cried Jimmy. "I can use electricity to get hydrogen out of water and it will be lighter than air. Then I can put it in Carl's inhaler, and we can do something really cool!"

$y = 3 \times 27$

$\sqrt{\dfrac{M}{12}}$

$x = y^2$

#

#

!

?

Carl took a big blast from his inhaler and then blew it out. He made the biggest nose bubble anyone had ever seen! All three boys began to rise up in the air, and the audience erupted in cheers.

"The winners of the annual Retroville Elementary School talent contest are . . . ," Miss Fowl said. "Oh, my. It's a tie!"

The boys heard the announcement just as they floated out the window and sailed up into the sky!

"Come back!" Miss Fowl shouted after them. "You forgot your trophy!"